RHYMES and RIDDLES
with
CORDUROY

Grosset & Dunlap

A bear's share of the royalties from the sale of
Rhymes and Riddles with Corduroy goes to the
Don and Lydia Freeman Research Fund to
support psychological care and research
concerning children with life-threatening illness.

Some material in this book was first published in *Corduroy's Christmas* in 1992, *Corduroy's Halloween* in 1995, *Corduroy's Birthday* in 1997, and *Corduroy's Easter* in 1999, by Viking Children's Books, a division of Penguin Putnam Books for Young Readers.

Library of Congress Cataloging-in-Publication Data is available.

ISBN 0-448-42655-2   A B C D E F G H I J

RHYMES and RIDDLES
with
CORDUROY

BASED ON THE CHARACTER CREATED BY DON FREEMAN

ILLUSTRATED BY LISA McCUE

Grosset & Dunlap, Publishers

A new year is starting!
What is the best month of the year?

January means snow—and snow means fun!
Skating and sledding for everyone!

What has two thumbs but no fingers?
A pair of mittens!

What's to love about **February**? Valentine's Day!
Let's have a party, make sweet treats, and play!

When does Valentine's Day come after Easter?
In the dictionary!

Puddles are everywhere in **March**! Splish-splash-splish!
Corduroy makes a rainy-day wish.

What goes up when rain comes down?
Umbrellas!

April brings us Easter and spring.
Egg hunts are more fun than anything!

What dessert is perfect for Easter?
Easter sundaes!

In **May**, flowers are everywhere.
That means spring is in the air!

What did spring say to winter?
Make like a tree and leave!

School is out! It's sunny today!
June means summer is on its way.

What can fly but has no wings?
A kite!

Strike up the band! Join in the fun!
Happy Fourth of **July** to everyone!

**What waves,
but has no hands?**
Our flag!

August is hot, so head for the beach.
Corduroy and his friends build a sand castle each!

What gets wetter the more it dries?
A towel!

Get ready for school, which starts in **September**.
There's so much to learn—and so much to remember!

What is the most curious letter of the alphabet?
The letter Y*!*

In **October**, the leaves are no longer green.
When the pumpkins come out, it's almost Halloween!

What did the ghost say to his girlfriend?
You look so boo-tiful!

In **November**, we make pumpkin pie.
Thanksgiving is here—is there snow in the sky?

What kind of music did Pilgrims like?
Plymouth Rock!

December! Snow is everywhere!
Christmas cheer is in the air!

What are filled in the morning and emptied
at night—except on Christmas?
Stockings!

We've gone through all the months,
so what happens then?
January is back!
Happy New Year again!

What's *your* favorite
month of the year?